This book about a big DRAGON

belongs to ...*Marco*...............

...................*Enjoy it!*...............

...................*Theo*...............

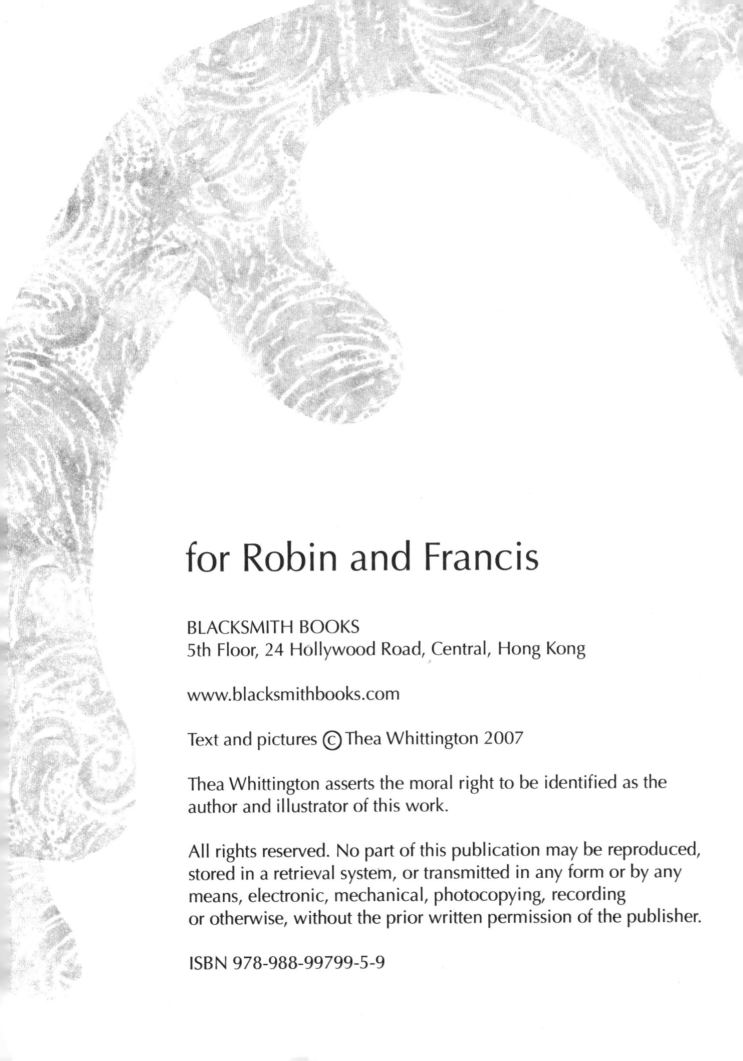

for Robin and Francis

BLACKSMITH BOOKS
5th Floor, 24 Hollywood Road, Central, Hong Kong

www.blacksmithbooks.com

ISBN 978-988-99799-5-9

The Dragon's Back

Thea Whittington

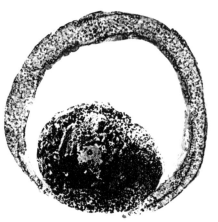

Siu Ming, his sister, his mum and dad
and their little dog lived in a large city
with tall buildings. It was a busy place,
but there were mountains and forests
nearby.

So one day they decided to go
for a special walk in the countryside.
Just before they started to walk
Siu Ming's dad got out a big map.

'You see that long red line - that
shows the path we will follow,'
he explained.

'The land looks a funny shape,'
thought Siu Ming,
but he said nothing.

Backbone's End

Pottinger
Gap

High Valley

Moun

Mount Parker

The Ridgeway

Pine

Limb Cove

High Peak

Headland View

Island Bay

The Lookout

Claw's Point

Rivermouth

They set off. It felt so lovely to walk through a big green space
after staying so long in the city. Siu Ming looked around him,
and at the large and rather jagged hills.

It didn't take long for him to realise that quite clearly
they were all on the back of an amazing and gigantic.....

....DRAGON!

'Wow!' exclaimed Siu Ming.

Then he wondered, 'But dad - is it a good dragon?'

His dad replied, 'Dragons are kind and bring good fortune.
People used to worship them because they brought rain
and helped the crops grow. People also thought that the green
dragons guarded part of the universe…. Dragons are very important.'

And so Siu Ming understood
that this dragon protected
the people who walked
on his back and enjoyed
the sand and sea by his sides.

Siu Ming and his family walked
on and on for over two hours.

'Time to stop for a snack!'
said Siu Ming's mum. 'It's hot
and it's been a hard climb.
But the view is wonderful.'

The air was getting quite heavy.

Siu Ming said, 'I can hear a little
thunder.' There was a sound of
faraway rumbling.

'The dragon is snoring,'
thought Siu Ming.

Suddenly he jumped up and
called, 'I can see....

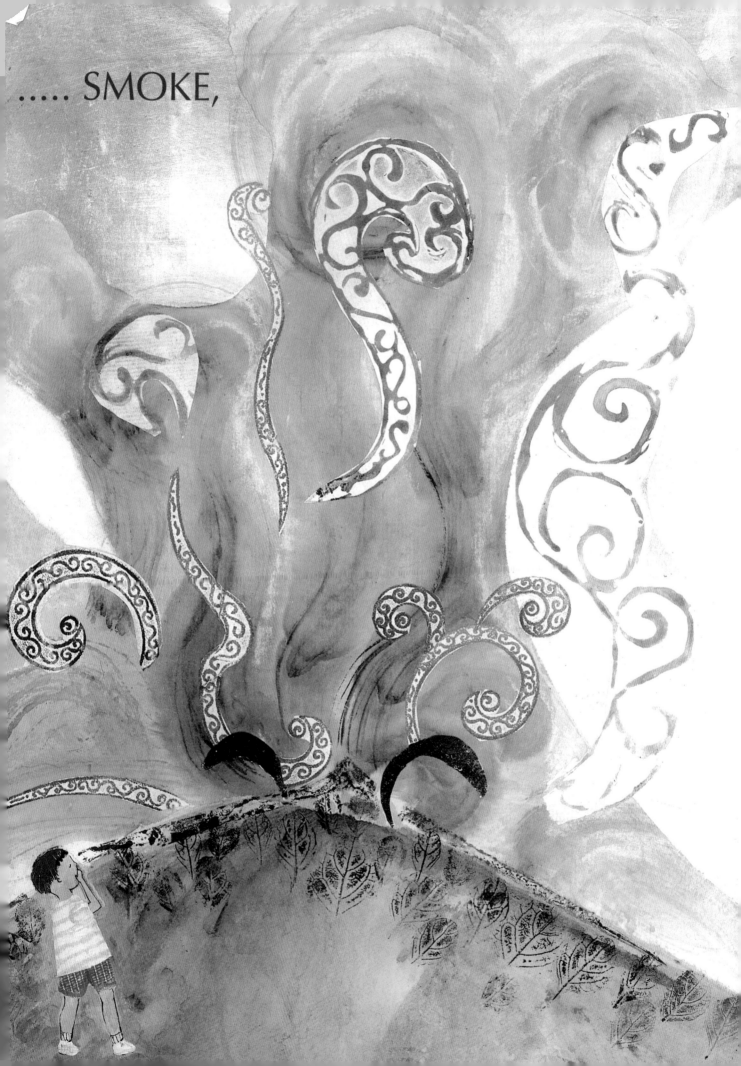

..... SMOKE,

FLAMES

and

FIRE!'

'We must get away!'
 the family all agreed.

'But we must rescue
 the poor dragon!'
 called Siu Ming.

'Hurry up!' begged his mother.

But Siu Ming kept looking back at where the dragon
was burning.

Then Siu Ming said
loudly,
'I can see a strange
object in the sea.

And I can hear....

A HELICOPTER!

It was hovering over the sea, and out from the bottom of the helicopter came a huge bucket. It scooped up seawater and afterwards....

....flew off towards the burning dragon.

Firemen rushed up the hillside carrying powerful hoses.

'These firemen are really good doctors for the dragon,' thought Siu Ming.

as he and his family watched water pouring from
the bucket and spraying from the long hoses.

But Siu Ming knew that the dragon was in a lot of pain.
The poor dragon sank his burning nostrils into the sea
and curled up his toes and dipped them into the water
so that he might feel a little better.

Siu Ming thought, 'The handsome green dragon is now
spoiled and he is very sad because something terrible
has happened to him. So he can no longer
protect all the people who enjoy walking on
his back.'

He could see that the dragon could hold back his tears
no longer. And the dragon just....

.... cried and cried.

The flames eventually died down until they were no more.

Siu Ming and his family were getting very wet. They had to leave.

Much later in the day Siu Ming and his dad came back to
a small edge of the dragon. Siu Ming asked,
'Dad, why was our dragon so terribly hurt?'

His dad sighed, 'When some people stopped to
light their delicious barbecues, they didn't care for him
as they should have done....'

'....and they left their barbecues burning!' cried Siu Ming.

'Yes', his dad replied.

'Will our dragon ever be green again?
Will the trees and flowers ever be as beautiful as they were
before the dragon caught fire?' Siu Ming asked.

'Well it will take a long time, but....'
And then his dad smiled, 'Yes, it will be lovely
here again. As long as people will care for the
land. You will always care for it, won't you?'

Siu Ming nodded. He wanted to care for
the dragon very much.

He wanted the trees and the plants to grow again,
for the dragon to be happy and full of life.

And so he waited.

The dragon did get better.

Then Siu Ming knew for sure that the dragon would always care for him, his family and anyone who came to walk or to play upon his back.

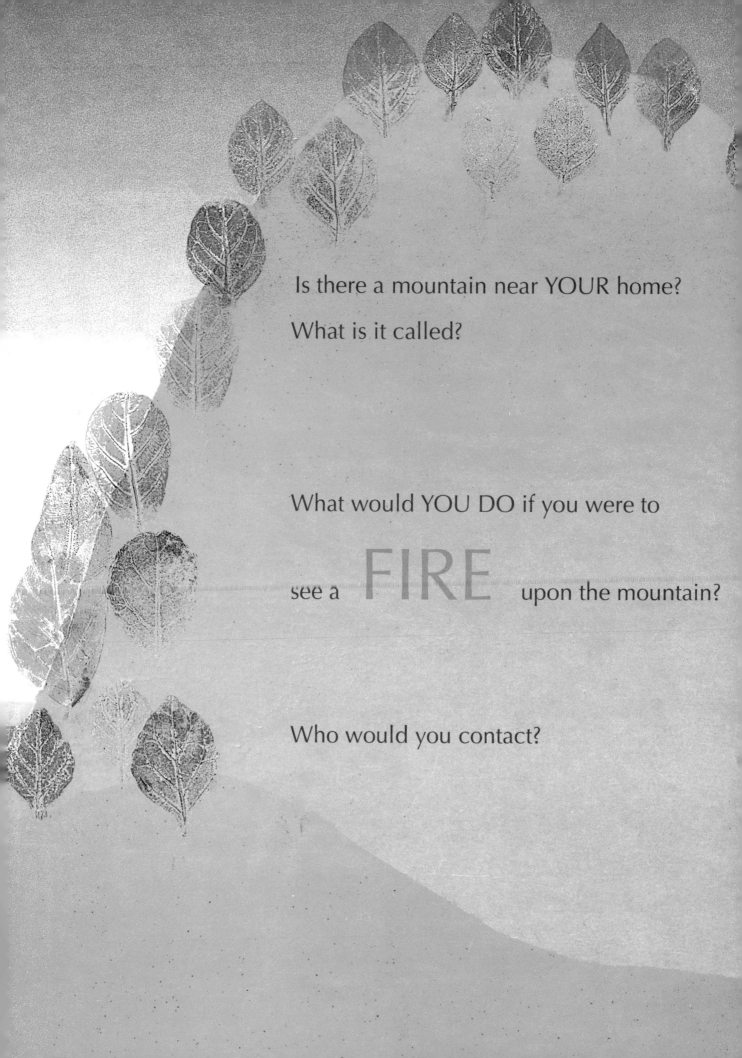

Is there a mountain near YOUR home?

What is it called?

What would YOU DO if you were to

see a   FIRE   upon the mountain?

Who would you contact?

You can make your own dragon!

You will need glue, scissors and wing screws.

Cut out the pieces and insert wing screws where you see ● so to attach the legs, tail, purple horns and blue breath to the body. (You may need an adult to help you with this). You can paint the screws green too if you wish. Tuck the wings of the screws under the dragon's body. Your dragon now has limbs which can waggle!

For the spikes on the spine and tail -

1. Bend the paper for the long spine and tail pieces outwards below the dotted lines.

2. Above the dotted lines glue together the 2 sides of the long spine and the 2 sides of the spikes on the waggly tail.

3. Stick the spikes along the appropriate dotted lines on your dragon

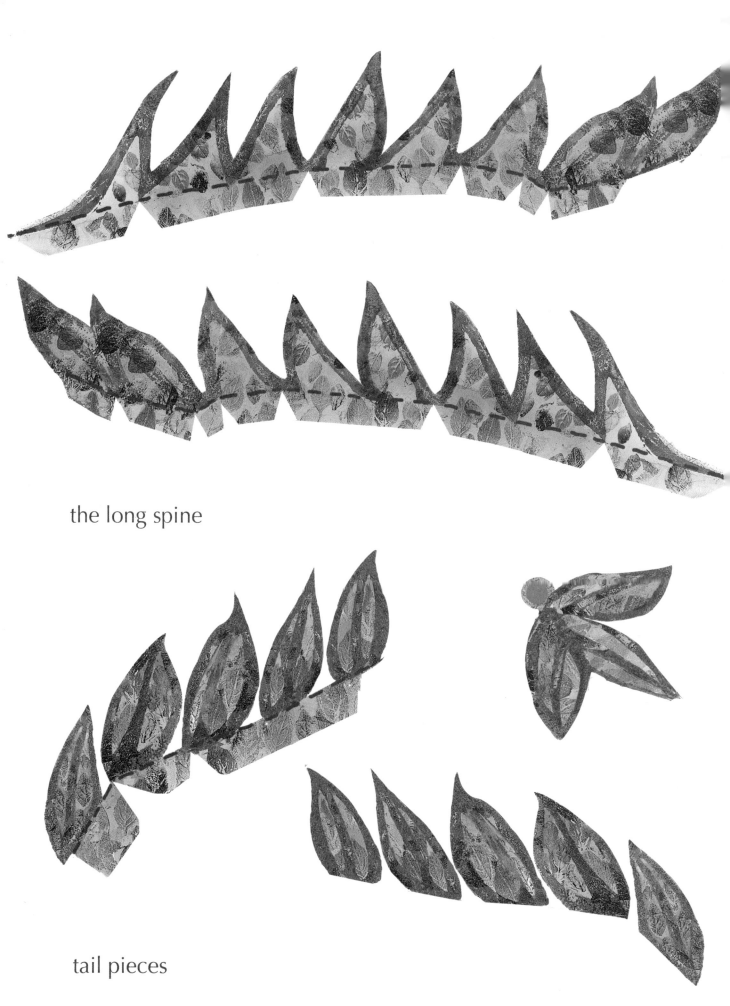

the long spine

tail pieces